ONE
SATURDAY
MORNING

by Barbara Baker
pictures by Kate Duke

Dutton Children's Books   New York

Library of Congress Cataloging-in-Publication Data

Baker, Barbara, date.
One Saturday morning/by Barbara Baker;
pictures by Kate Duke.—1st ed.
p.   cm.
Summary: One Saturday a family enjoys such activities as getting up
one by one, going to the park, and eating spaghetti for lunch.
ISBN 0-525-45262-1
[1. Family life—Fiction.]   I. Duke, Kate, ill.   II. Title.
PZ7.B16922On   1994   [E]—dc20   93-43957   CIP   AC

Published in the United States 1994 by Dutton Children's Books,
a division of Penguin Books USA Inc.
375 Hudson Street, New York, New York 10014
Printed in Hong Kong
First Edition
10 9 8 7 6 5 4

For Jim, Susan, and Kate Baker
B.A.B.

CONTENTS

MAMA

One Saturday morning

Mama woke up early.

It was very quiet.

"Good," said Mama to herself.

"Papa is asleep.

Lily is asleep.

Rose and Daisy are asleep.

And Jack is asleep.

I can stay in bed.

How nice."

Just then, Papa opened his eyes.

"Hello, Mama," he said.

"Is it time to get up?"

"Shhh," said Mama.

"Lily is asleep.

Rose and Daisy are asleep.

Jack is asleep.

We can stay in bed."

"How nice," said Papa.

"What is nice?" said Lily

from the doorway.

"Shhh," said Mama.

"Rose and Daisy are asleep.

Jack is asleep.

We can stay in bed."

Lily got into bed

with Mama and Papa.

"This is fun," said Lily.

Rose and Daisy came

into the room.

"What is fun?" said Rose.

"Shhh," said Lily.

"Jack is asleep.

We can stay in bed."

Rose and Daisy jumped

into the big bed.

They hugged Mama and Papa.

"Me, me," said Jack

from the doorway.

Mama helped Jack into the bed.

Then Mama got up.

She went into the kitchen.

It was quiet.

Mama made a cup of tea.

She made some toast and

put some jam on it.

She sat down.

"How nice," said Mama.

LILY

"Hello, Mama," said Lily.

Mama was eating toast with jam.

"Hello, Lily," she said.

"Would you like some toast?"

"Yes, please," said Lily.

She sat down at the table

with Mama.

It was quiet in the kitchen.

The toast smelled good.

Mama gave Lily a cup

with a little tea in it

and a lot of milk.

"Thank you," said Lily.

She smiled at Mama.

They ate their toast

and sipped their tea.

They could hear Papa

and Rose and Daisy and Jack

in the bedroom.

"They are playing a noisy game,"

Lily told Mama.

"But I wanted to be quiet with you."

Mama and Lily finished

their toast and tea.

"That was nice," said Mama.

Papa came into the kitchen.

Rose and Daisy and Jack came, too.

"What was nice?" said Papa.

Lily smiled at Mama.

"Toast with jam," said Lily,

"is very, very nice."

19

ROSE

Rose loved toast with jam.

"More toast, please," she said.

But no one listened.

Mama and Papa were

washing the dishes.

Lily was reading a book.

Daisy was singing to her doll.

And Jack was playing

with the telephone.

"More toast, please,"

said Rose again.

But still no one listened.

"I WANT MORE TOAST!"

screamed Rose.

Everybody stopped.

"*Rose!*" said Mama.

"That is *no* way to ask

for something."

So Rose began to cry.

But no one listened because

Papa dropped a dish.

And Mama heard Jack

playing with the telephone.

Lily went back to her book.

And Daisy sang louder to her doll.

Rose cried and cried.

Finally Papa and Mama

came to her.

"What is the matter, Rose?"

said Papa.

"Please tell us,"

said Mama.

So Rose told them.

"I want more toast," she said.

"I did say 'please.'

But nobody would listen to me."

"Oh, dear," said Mama.

Then Papa made some toast.

Mama put jam on it.

And Rose ate every bite.

DAISY

Daisy was singing

to her baby doll.

"Who wants to go to the park?"

said Papa.

Everybody wanted to go.

So Papa put on his favorite

Saturday morning hat.

"I'm ready," he said.

"Wait for me!" cried Daisy.

She got her new carriage.

"Oh, Daisy," said Papa.

"Do you really need the carriage?"

"Yes," said Daisy. "I do."

She put her doll into it

and covered her with a blanket.

On the way to the park,

Lily and Rose ran ahead.

Daisy walked slowly with her carriage.

Papa helped her up and down curbs.

"Here we are," said Papa.

He sat down on a bench.

Mama put Jack in the sandbox.

Daisy pushed her carriage

back and forth.

Lily and Rose climbed

to the top of the slide.

"Look at us," they yelled.

Daisy found a pebble.

She put it in her carriage

for her baby doll.

Lily and Rose ran over to the swings.

Daisy found a gray feather.

She put it in her carriage

for her baby doll.

"Jack is eating sand!" cried Mama.

Papa ran to stop him.

Daisy pushed her carriage by.

"My baby doesn't eat sand," she said.

Lily and Rose played tag.

Daisy found a small stick.

She put it in her carriage

for her baby doll.

"It's time to go," called Papa.

Lily and Rose ran ahead.

Daisy pushed her carriage home.

Papa opened the front door.

Then he stopped.

"Oh, no!" he said. "I lost my hat."

"Oh, dear," said Mama.

But Daisy smiled.

She took her doll out of her carriage.

Then she took out—

one pebble,

one gray feather,

one small stick, and...

34

Papa's favorite Saturday morning hat.

"SURPRISE!" cried Daisy.

"Oh, thank you, Daisy," said Papa.

"You *did* need your carriage."

"Yes," said Daisy. "I did."

JACK

Mama took Jack out of his stroller.

"No!" said Jack.

"He must be tired," said Papa.

"No," said Jack.

"He must be hungry," said Lily.

"No," said Jack.

Mama put Jack in his high chair.

Then she went to make lunch.

"No, no, no," said Jack.

Mama gave Jack some cheese.

"No," said Jack.

He pushed it away.

"I'll eat it," said Rose.

She took the cheese.

"NO!" Jack screamed.

He started to cry.

"Rose," said Mama,

"please go wash your hands."

Rose went to wash her hands.

Mama gave Jack more cheese.

"No," said Jack.

But he stopped crying.

"No, no, no," he sang.

Mama smiled at Jack.

"No," said Jack.

But he smiled at Mama.

Then he played with his cheese

until lunch was ready.

PAPA

"Mmmm, spaghetti," said Papa.

"My favorite lunch."

He twirled some spaghetti

on his fork.

He opened his mouth.

"Help!" said Daisy.

"My spaghetti is too long."

"I'm helping Jack," said Mama.

So Papa put his fork down.

He cut Daisy's spaghetti.

He picked his fork up.

"No fair," said Rose.

"Daisy has more than I do."

Papa put his fork down.

He gave Rose more spaghetti.

He picked his fork up.

"Papa," said Lily,

"show me how to twirl mine."

"Okay," said Papa. "Watch me."

He twirled some spaghetti

on his fork.

He opened his mouth.

"*Ouch!*" yelled Rose.

"My spaghetti is too hot."

Papa put his fork down.

He stirred Rose's spaghetti to cool it.

"Daisy spilled her milk," said Lily.

Papa cleaned up the spill.

"I need more milk," said Daisy.

"And I need more spaghetti," said Lily.

"And I do, too," said Rose.

"No," said Jack.

Papa helped everyone.

Finally Lily and Rose

and Daisy and Jack

were finished.

Papa looked at his plate.

It was full of cold spaghetti.

"Don't worry," said Mama.

She took Papa's plate away.

She filled it with hot spaghetti.

"Thank you," said Papa.

He picked up his fork.

He twirled some spaghetti

and put it into his mouth.

"Mmmm, spaghetti," said Papa.

"My favorite lunch."